A DOLPHIN DAY IN HAWAII

Written and illustrated

By

Dennis Asato

Printed in Thailand

By Darnsutha Press Co.,Ltd.

Published by Anoai Press

ISBN: 0-9653971-8-1

Distributed by
Anoai Press
3349-A Anoai Place
Honolulu, Hawaii 96822
USA
Phone: (808) 988-6109
Fax: (808) 988-1119
E Mail: kukui@lava.net
Anoai Press Web page:
http://www.anoaipress.com/

A DOLPHIN DAY

IN HAWAII

written and illustrated
by dennis asato

Very early,
one bright, beautiful morning,
I went to the beach
to catch a few waves.

When I got to the shore,
I saw something in the water.

"OH NO, IT'S A SHARK!
I DON'T THINK I SHOULD GO
IN THE WATER TODAY."
I said to myself
and started to leave.

As I was leaving, I heard something go,

"Wheeeeeeeeeeeeeeeeeeeeeeeeeeee!"
Then I looked out on the ocean
and saw that it was not a shark,
it was a dolphin!

A dolphin riding a wave!

"Wheeeeeeeeeeeeeeeeeeee!"
The Dolphin caught another wave.

"DOLPHINS ARE SUPPOSED TO BE FRIENDLY."
I said to myself.
"I WONDER IF WE CAN BE FRIENDS AND PLAY?"

Then I got an idea.

Further up on the beach,
I remembered,
there were some white ginger plants
that were flowering today.

I paddled my surfboard
out to where the dolphin was
and.....................................

 "Mmmmmmmmmmmmmm."

"Hello." The dolphin said.
"Thank you soooo much for sharing those flowers with me.
They smell wonderful!"

"YOU'RE A DOLPHIN, AREN'T YOU?" I asked.

"Uh huh." the dolphin answered. "And you're a....???"

"A BEAR." I replied.

"Oh, you're a bear!" said the dolphin. "Wanna play?"

"YES!" I answered eagerly.

"Hop on my back." the dolphin said. _AND OFF WE WENT._

 "WHAAAAAEEEEEEEHOOOOOOOOOOO!!!!!"

We leaped out of the water
and swam faster than I ever went.

"WOOOOOOOOOOOOOOOOOOOOOOOOO!"

Then the dolphin showed me
the best places
to see the colorful fishes of the reef.

I saw butterfly fish,
balloon fish,
squirrel fish,
parrot fish,
goat fish,
all kinds of wonderful sealife.

"NOW," I said, "IT'S MY TURN
TO SHOW YOU THE THINGS ON LAND."

The dolphin's skin
had to be kept wet all the time
so I was sure to bring along
a water spray.

As we headed inland, the dolphin said,
"What's that beautiful sound?"

"THAT'S A BIRD." I said
"LET'S ASK THE BIRD TO SING FOR US."

I told the bird that this was
the dolphin's first journey to see the land.

"COULD YOU SING A SONG
FOR THE DOLPHIN AND ME?"
I asked the bird.

The bird
was so happy
to sing for us.

The song of the bird
was like the beautiful things of the earth.
It touched our hearts.

The bird finished the song,
gave a little bow,
and flew up into the trees.

"THank you," we said.
"we RealLy EnjoyeD the song."

Then the dolphin said,

"What wonderful things trees are.
They're so beautiful and green,
they shade us from the sun,
and they give the birds a place to stay."

The dolphin wanted to know
the names of the trees and birds.
Dolphins are very smart.

"THAT'S A MANGO TREE,
THAT'S A SPARROW,
THAT'S A COCONUT TREE,
THAT'S A MYNAHBIRD."
I named as many as I could.

I realized that I didn't know
the names of many trees and birds that I saw every day.
I told myself to go to the library someday
and learn more about all the trees and birds.

Then I took the dolphin to a tree
that liked to play with everyone.

The dolphin enjoyed swinging.
Dolphins love to have fun.

The dolphin insisted
that I ride on the swing next.
The dolphin was very thoughtful.
It was the first time
that I was ever pushed by flukes.
That's what they call
the tail part of the dolphin.

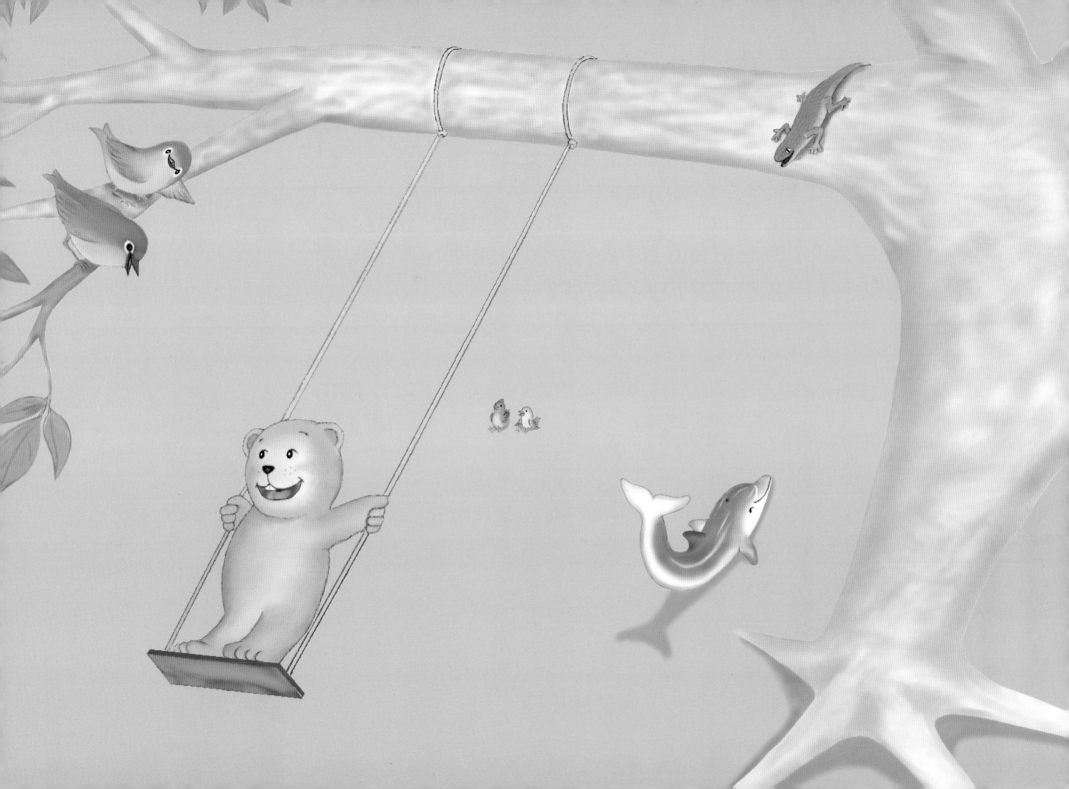

After we finished with the swing,
I shared all the bear jokes
that I could remember with the dolphin.
The dolphin told me a few good dolphin jokes, too,
and we laughed and laughed.

We had a wonderful, warm feeling in our chests
from all the fun we had
and from the song of the bird.

As we sat there, we enjoyed the sounds
of all the different kinds of birds around us.

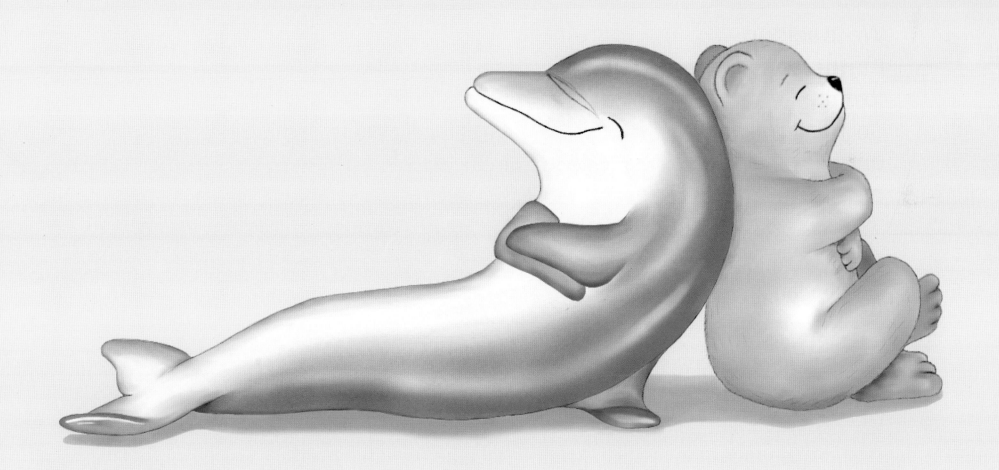

We decided
that it was a great idea
to take a short nap
on the fine grass,
under the shade
of a large green tree.

When we woke up from our nap,
the dolphin had to go back to the ocean
for it was getting late.

As we got to the seashore
where we began our trip into the land,
the dolphin said,

"Please tell the people of the land
that they are making the oceans dirty
and that all the creatures in the sea
cannot live if the ocean gets dirtier."

I said I would.

We both thanked each other
for such a wonderful day.
We felt like old friends
who knew each other
for a long, long time.

"I'll be back again." the dolphin called.

"GREAT! WE'LL HAVE MORE FUN." I answered.

Out in the sea,
family and friends were happy to see
that the dolphin was returning and fine.

It was quite late,
so I hurried home
before my family worried about me, too.

That was the end of my first
DOLPHIN DAY.

ABOUT THE AUTHOR

Dennis Asato has authored and illustrated several children's books. Professionally Dennis uses computer technology to design building mechanical systems for engineering firms in Honolulu. Combining that technology with his love of art, the illustrations for *A Dolphin Day In Hawaii* and *Mama Is Hapai*, were created by computer.

Dennis has a bachelor's degree in psychology and sociology. His special interest is transpersonal psychology. Besides being an artist, he is also a musician and plays the guitar.